DANIEL TIGER'S NEIGHBORHOOD

My Family Is Special

Adapted by Maggie Testa
Based on the screenplay "Family Day"
written by Jennifer Hamburg
Poses and layouts by Jason Fruchter

Ready-to-Read

Simon Spotlight
New York   London   Toronto   Sydney   New Delhi

SIMON SPOTLIGHT
An imprint of Simon & Schuster Children's Publishing Division
1230 Avenue of the Americas, New York, New York 10020
This Simon Spotlight edition August 2020
© 2020 The Fred Rogers Company. All rights reserved.
All rights reserved, including the right of reproduction in whole or in part in any form.
SIMON SPOTLIGHT, READY-TO-READ, and colophon are registered trademarks of Simon & Schuster, Inc.
For information about special discounts for bulk purchases, please contact Simon & Schuster Special
Sales at 1-866-506-1949 or business@simonandschuster.com.
Manufactured in the United States of America 0720 LAK
2 4 6 8 10 9 7 5 3 1
ISBN 978-1-5344- 6982-2 (hc)
ISBN 978-1-5344-6981-5 (pb)
ISBN 978-1-5344-6983-9 (eBook)

Hi, neighbor!

Today is family day.

I will make a tree branch with a picture of my family on it.

Jodi is making her branch.

There is a leaf for her, one for her mama, two for her brothers, and one for her nana.

All families

are different.

Prince Wednesday
is making
his branch.

There is a leaf for him,
one for his dad,
one for his mom,
and one for his brother.

All families
are different.

Find what makes your family special!

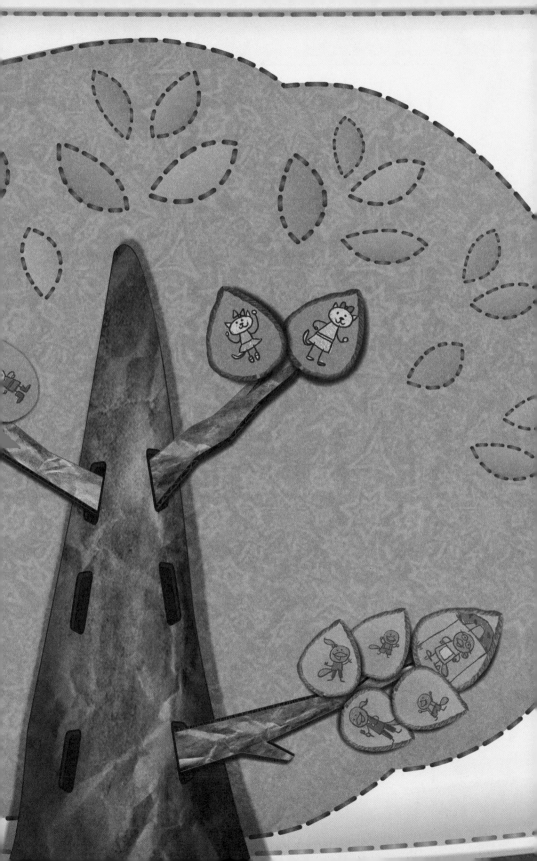

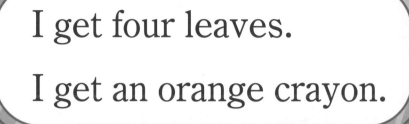

I get four leaves.

I get an orange crayon.

I draw my dad, my mom,

myself, and baby Margaret.

O is making his branch.

He grabs a blue crayon.

O and his uncle X
have blue feathers.

Miss Elaina is making her branch.

She needs more than one color to draw her family.

All families are different.
Find what makes
your family special!

Uncle X and Miss Elaina
put their branches
on the tree.

They talk about

what makes

their families special.

But what makes my family special?

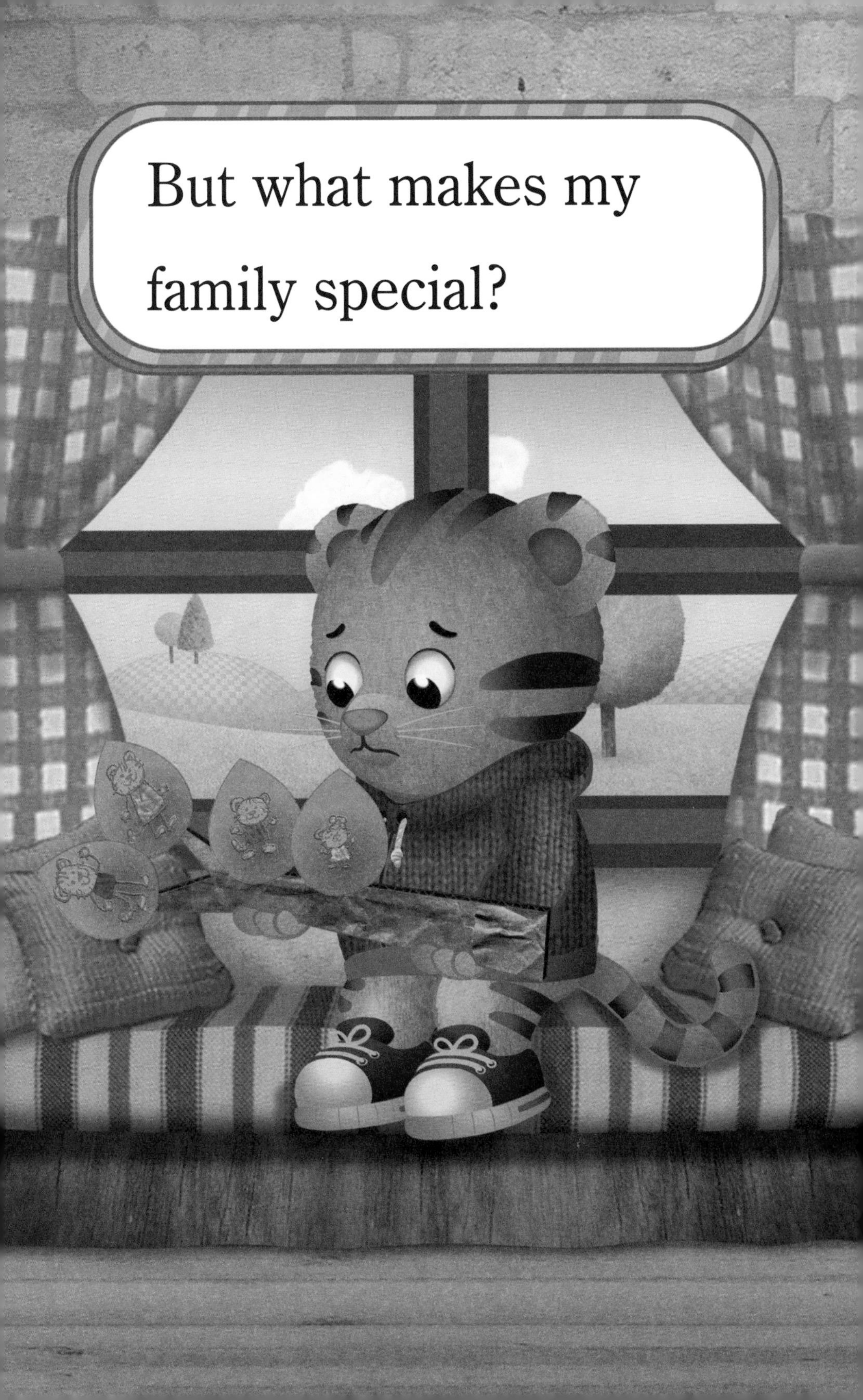

All families are different.
Find what makes
your family special!

What are some special things about your family? Ugga Mugga!